For Gontdawgie,
the Woman who flew away

First published in 1999

3 5 7 9 10 8 6 4 2

First published in the United Kingdom in 1999 by
Hutchinson Children's Books
Random House UK Limited
20 Vauxhall Bridge Road, London SW1V 2SA

Random House Australia (Pty) Limited
20 Alfred Street, Milsons Point, Sydney
New South Wales 2061, Australia

Random House New Zealand Limited
18 Poland Road, Glenfield
Auckland 10, New Zealand

Random House South Africa (Pty) Limited
Endulini, 5A Jubilee Road, Parktown 2193, South Africa

Random House UK Limited Reg. No. 954009

A CIP catalogue record for this book is available from the British Library

ISBN 0 09 176628 1

Printed in Singapore

The
WONDERFUL
JOURNEY

Paul Geraghty

HUTCHINSON

London Sydney Auckland Johannesburg

My grandma came to live with us from a long way away. Every Wednesday she took me to the railway yard to see the trains. If it rained, we sat in an empty shack beside the railway. And there, to the smell of steel and the shudder of the engines, she would tell me stories from the far away places she used to live.

One day she told me a true story.

'Do you remember,' she said, 'the time I told you that I would fly away?'

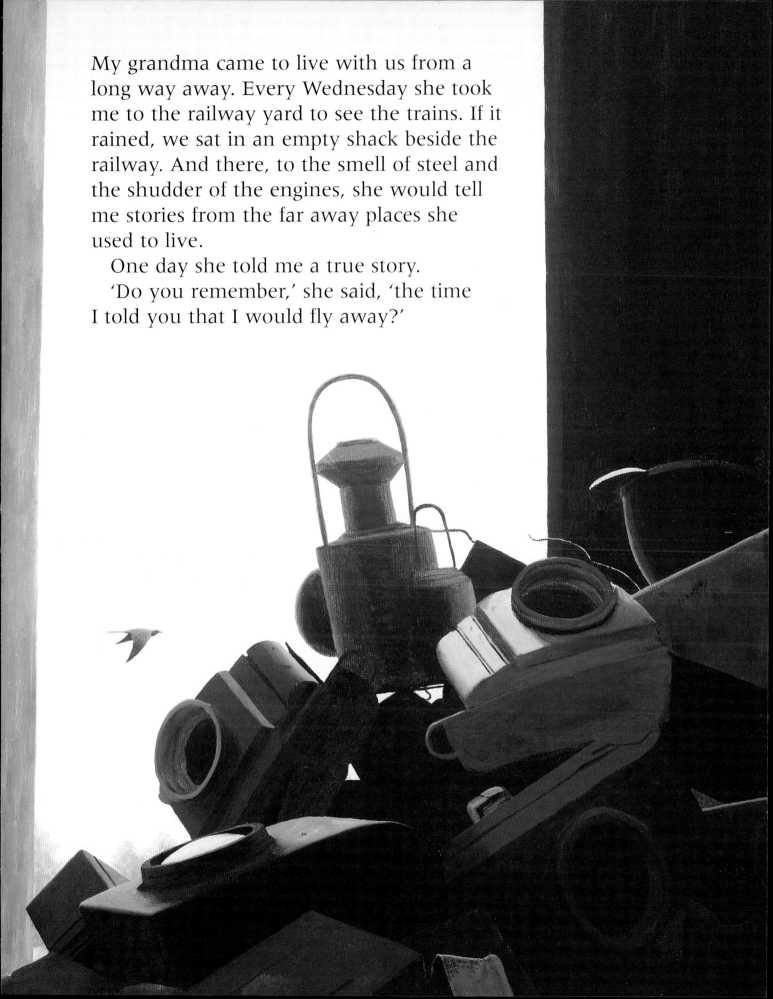

I remembered. She had been telling me about the place where she was born. She seemed to be looking a long way past the sun. 'One day,' she had sighed, 'I will fly back home to where I came from. And then I will be happy.'

I knew she could fly.

'Aren't you happy here?' I asked her.

'Not really,' she'd said, but she never told me why.

'Well,' said Gran, 'that time has come.
Time for me to fly away.'
'But you can't go,' I cried.
'Time doesn't stand still,'
she said. 'I can't
stay forever.'

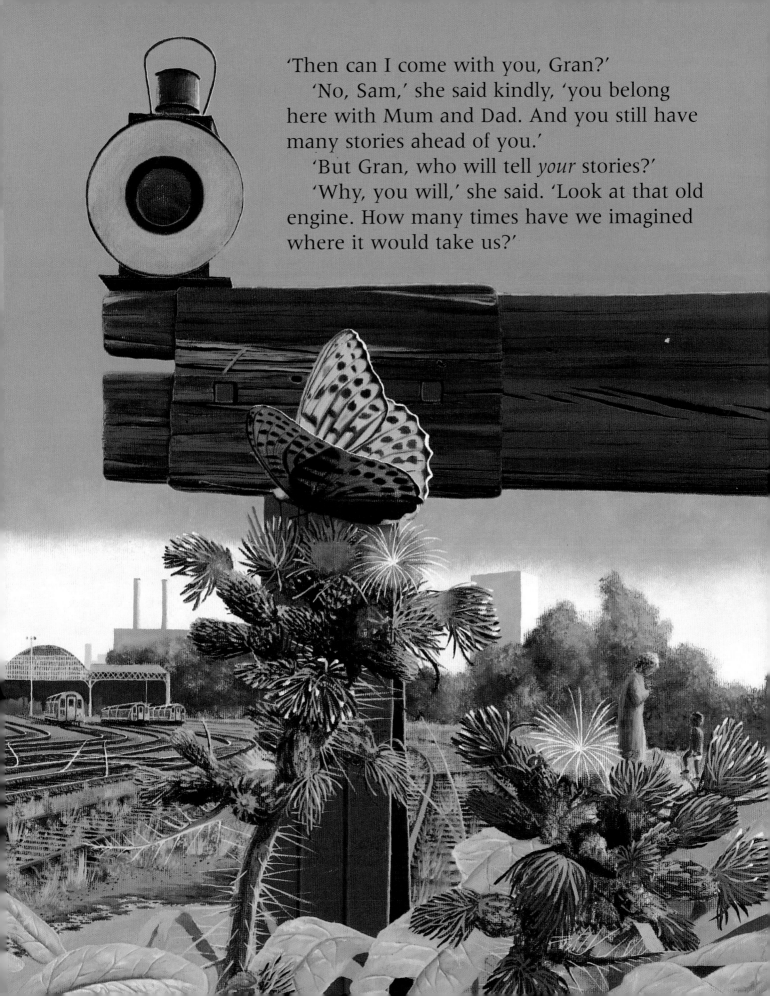

'Then can I come with you, Gran?'

'No, Sam,' she said kindly, 'you belong here with Mum and Dad. And you still have many stories ahead of you.'

'But Gran, who will tell *your* stories?'

'Why, you will,' she said. 'Look at that old engine. How many times have we imagined where it would take us?'

'Besides, you can still see me if I go away,' she went on. 'You can see me from the other side of the world, whenever you want!'

I laughed at her. 'People can't see *that* far.'

'Oh, but they can,' said Gran. 'Didn't you know?'

When she told me that, I felt a tingle run down my neck, right to my toes.

'Would you like to see Africa right now?' she whispered.

We closed our eyes and she told me a story: we were flamingos, flying high across the sky.

Over the sea we flew, above green mountains and a hot, baking desert, till we were too tired and thirsty to go on. So we rested with the other birds in our favourite steamy lake.

'Not long now,' said Gran, 'till our migration is over.'

And off we went again, this time high over villages, rivers and forests until vast open plains appeared below.

We landed near a pride of lions, resting beneath knotty trees and a great volcanic mountain.

'We are now very close to where I used to live,' Gran whispered. 'The sun met me every morning and the sound of the animals sent me to sleep at night.'

I wanted to go there. I wanted to look back and see if I could see Gran from the mountain.

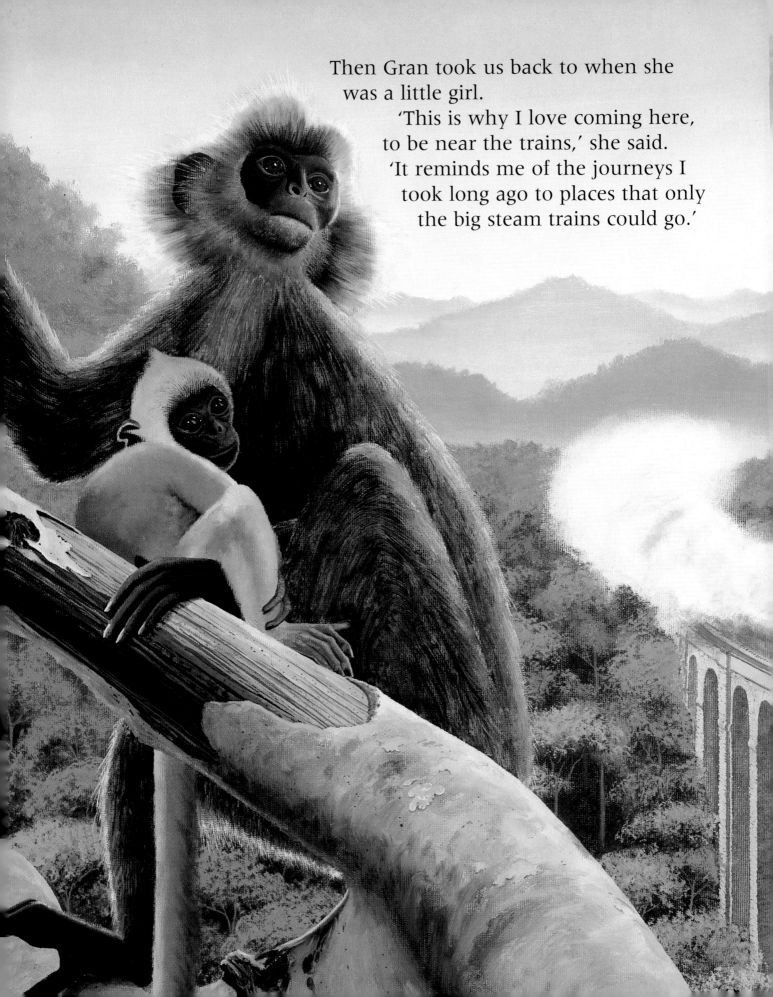

Then Gran took us back to when she
was a little girl.
'This is why I love coming here,
to be near the trains,' she said.
'It reminds me of the journeys I
took long ago to places that only
the big steam trains could go.'

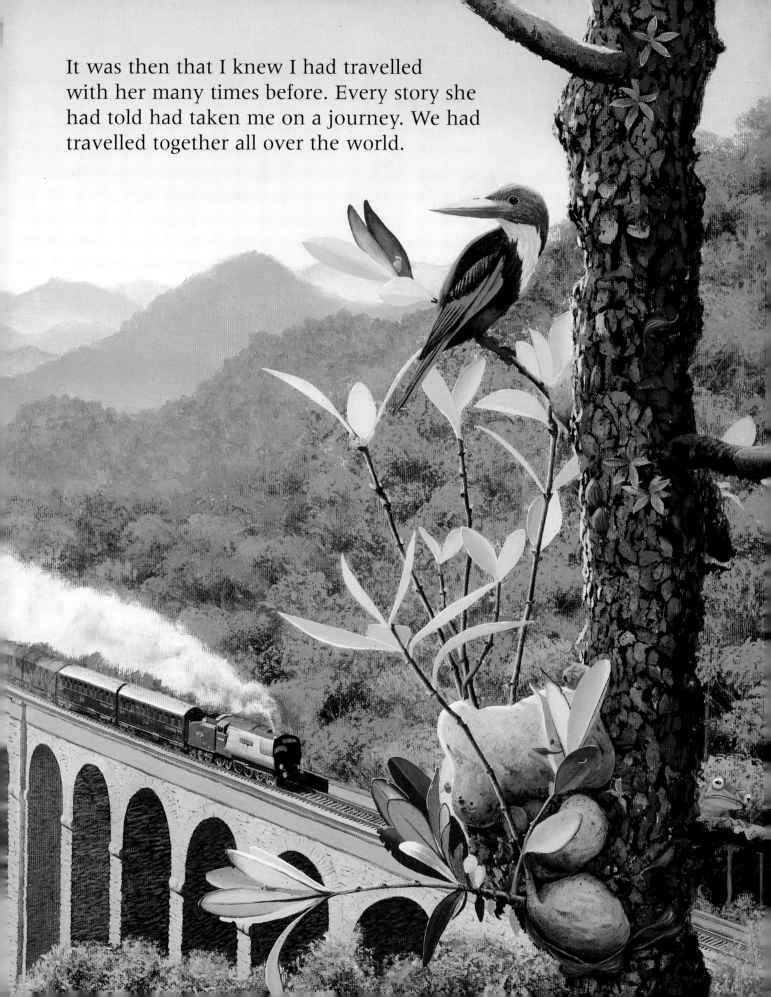

It was then that I knew I had travelled with her many times before. Every story she had told had taken me on a journey. We had travelled together all over the world.

'So you see,' said Gran, 'you can travel any time you want, anywhere you wish.' She looked up at the sky. It was getting late. 'And right now I think we'd better travel home!'

I felt scared. I didn't want to go, in case I never saw her again.

'Don't be silly!' she laughed. 'Just remember, you can see me whenever you like.'

Then she gave me a big hug. 'This is our special goodbye,' she said.

That night I travelled on my own to strange, and wonderful places that I had never seen before. I knew then that I would always be able to reach Gran, wherever she went. And that she would always be able to reach me.

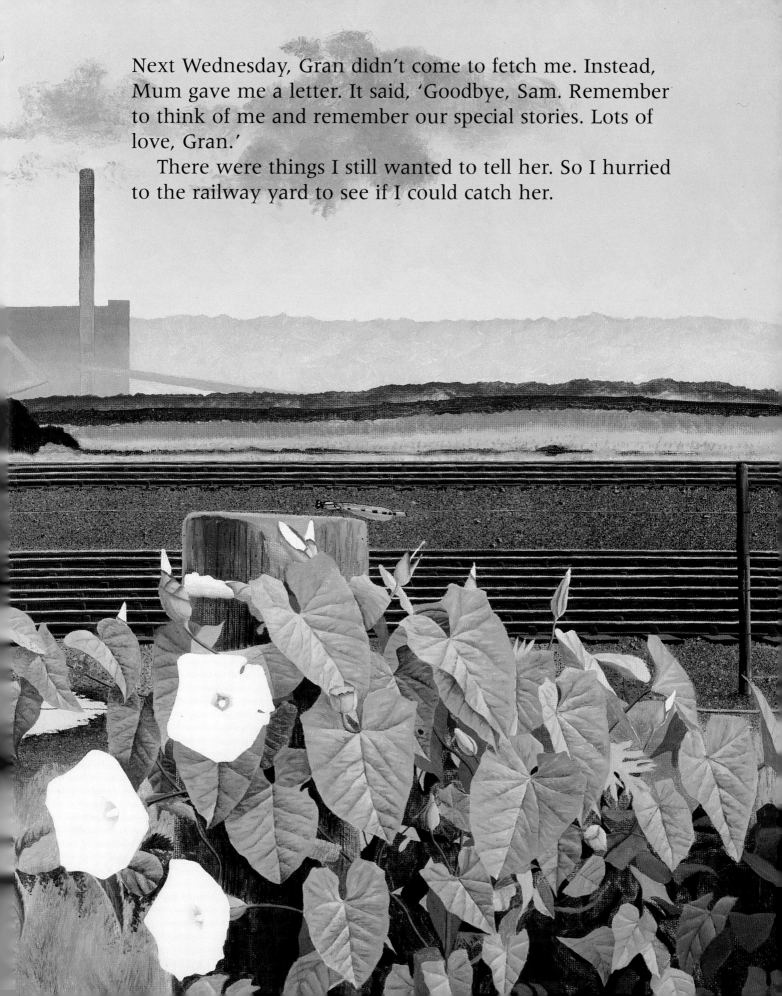

Next Wednesday, Gran didn't come to fetch me. Instead, Mum gave me a letter. It said, 'Goodbye, Sam. Remember to think of me and remember our special stories. Lots of love, Gran.'

There were things I still wanted to tell her. So I hurried to the railway yard to see if I could catch her.

I looked in the shack where we had sheltered. I couldn't find Gran, but everywhere I looked were the stories we had shared.

Gran had flown away. But in the thunder of the trains, I could still hear her voice.